MAIN LIBRARY
ALBANY PUBLIC LIBRARY

 T5-COE-206

Weekend Fun

Let's Go to a Movie

By Mary Hill

Children's Press®
A Division of Scholastic Inc.
New York / Toronto / London / Auckland / Sydney
Mexico City / New Delhi / Hong Kong
Danbury, Connecticut

Thanks to Clearview's Anthony Wayne in Wayne, PA
Thanks to Ritz Theater Group in Philadelphia, PA

Photo Credits: All images by Maura B. McConnell
Contributing Editors: Shira Laskin and Jennifer Silate
Book Design: Michael DeLisio

Library of Congress Cataloging-in-Publication Data

Hill, Mary, 1977-
   Let's go to a movie / by Mary Hill.
   p. cm.—(Weekend fun)
   Includes index.
   Summary: Describes the experiences of a young boy and his mother when they go to a theater to see a movie.
   ISBN 0-516-23999-6 (lib. bdg.) ISBN 0-516-25917-2 (pbk.)
   1. Motion pictures—Juvenile literature. [1. Motion pictures.] I. Title. II. Series.

PN1994.5.H496 2003
791.43—dc21

2003009156

Copyright © 2004 Rosen Book Works, Inc. All rights reserved.
Published in 2004 by Children's Press, an imprint of Scholastic Library Publishing.
Published simultaneously in Canada.
Printed in the United States of America.
1 2 3 4 5 6 7 8 9 10 R 13 12 11 10 09 08 07 06 05 04

MAR 2 9 2005

MAIN LIBRARY
ALBANY PUBLIC LIBRARY

Contents

1. Going to the Movies — 4
2. Box Office — 6
3. The Movie — 14
4. New Words — 22
5. To Find Out More — 23
6. Index — 24
7. About the Author — 24

My name is Jorge.

My mom and I are going to the movies.

We must buy **tickets** to see the movie.

Mom will buy our tickets at the **box office**.

A man takes my ticket when we enter the **movie theater**.

There is a **snack bar** in the theater.

We can buy popcorn to eat during the movie.

Mom buys us some popcorn and some soda.

The popcorn tastes good!

It is time for the movie to start.

Mom and I go into the theater to get our seats.

Mom and I find seats.

I like to sit close to the **screen**.

The lights are turned off when the movie starts.

Everyone is quiet while the movie is playing.

The movie is over.

I liked it a lot!

New Words

box office (**bahks ahf**-is) the ticket office at a theater

movie theater (**moo**-vee **thee**-uh-tuhr) a building where movies are shown

screen (**skreen**) a white surface on which movies are shown

snack bar (**snak bahr**) a place where people can buy things to eat and drink

tickets (**tik**-its) small pieces of paper that show you have paid for something

To Find Out More

Book
At the Movie Theater
by Sandy Francis
Child's World

Web Sites
Kids First!
http://www.cqcm.org/kidsfirst/home.shtml
Looking for a good movie to see? This Web site will help you and your parents choose a movie that is fun to watch and made just for kids!

PBS: Nova: Special Effects
http://www.pbs.org/wgbh/nova/specialfx
Learn how special effects are made for some of your favorite movies on this Web site.

Index

box office, 6

lights, 18

movie
   theater, 8

popcorn, 10, 12

screen, 16
snack bar, 10
soda, 12

ticket, 6, 8

About the Author
Mary Hill has written many books for children. For fun on the weekends, she likes to go sailing.

Reading Consultants

Kris Flynn, Coordinator, Small School District Literacy, The San Diego County Office of Education

Shelly Forys, Certified Reading Recovery Specialist, W.J. Zahnow Elementary School, Waterloo, IL

Paulette Mansell, Certified Reading Recovery Specialist, and Early Literacy Consultant, TX